Popcorn
the Wonder Pony

OUTWOOD PRIMARY
SCHOOL

Story by Jill McDougall
Illustrations by Mark Guthrie

NELSON
A Cengage Company

Popcorn the Wonder Pony

Text: Jill McDougall
Series consultant: Annette Smith
Publishing editor: Simone Calderwood
Editor: Annabel Smith
Designer: Kerri Wilson
Series designers: James Lowe and
   Karen Mayo
Illustrations: Mark Guthrie
Production controller: Erin Dowling
Reprint: Siew Han Ong

PM Guided Reading

Emerald Level 25

Moving On
Famous Bridges
Hector's Electro-Pet Shop
The Arctic Circle
The Swimming Pool Project
Making Art with Light
Alex the Super Soccer Striker
The Great Barrier Reef
Popcorn the Wonder Pony
A Community Cares and Shares

Text © 2015 Cengage Learning Australia Pty Limited
Illustrations © 2015 Cengage Learning Australia Pty Limited

ISBN 978 0 17 036897 1

Cengage Learning Australia
Level 7, 80 Dorcas Street
South Melbourne, Victoria Australia 3205
Phone: 1300 790 853

Cengage Learning New Zealand
Unit 4B Rosedale Office Park
331 Rosedale Road, Albany, North Shore NZ 0632
Phone: 0800 449 725

For learning solutions, visit **cengage.com.au**

Printed in Singapore by 1010 Printing Group Limited
4 5 6 7 19 18

Contents

Chapter 1   Joining the Pony Club   4

Chapter 2   Too Many Tricks!   9

Chapter 3   The First Event   14

Chapter 4   Cheers for Popcorn   19

Chapter 5   Popcorn's Last Chance   25

Chapter 6   Popcorn, the Superstar   29

Chapter 1
Joining the Pony Club

"Welcome to the Silver Saddles Pony Club!" said Mrs Hambone, the riding teacher. She smiled at me. "You have a lovely pony, Sophie. What's his name?"

"Popcorn," I told her.

The other girls looked at Popcorn with surprise.

"Why does Popcorn have gold stars on his saddle?" asked a girl on a grey pony.

I stroked Popcorn's sleek neck. "Because Popcorn is a superstar," I told the girl.

Everyone laughed. I could tell that they didn't believe me.

ver Saddles
Pony Club

Popcorn really was a star. In fact, Popcorn and I used to do tricks in our family circus. Popcorn was called "Popcorn the Wonder Pony".

After Mum and Dad sold the circus, Mum suggested we join the pony club, because Popcorn seemed bored with nothing to do all day. I hoped Popcorn the Wonder Pony would fit in with all the other ponies.

"First, we will walk around the ring," said Mrs Hambone.

Popcorn and I followed the others into the ring. Popcorn seemed excited. He flicked his ears and swished his tail. He thought we were about to perform one of our tricks.

"Everybody walk slowly," ordered Mrs Hambone. "Then, turn around and walk the other way."

Round and around the ring we went with all the other ponies. Then we turned and went the other way.

I leaned forward and stroked Popcorn's neck. "Good boy," I said, trying not to yawn.

I was sure Popcorn was trying not to yawn, too. I knew he would much prefer to be doing tricks. Popcorn loved to hear people cheering and clapping for him.

"Now you may trot," called Mrs Hambone.

I loosened the reins and nudged Popcorn's soft belly with my knees. He broke into a trot and we kept going round the circle behind the other ponies. I looked at the other riders. Everyone else seemed to be bored, too.

Suddenly, I had an idea.

"Get ready, boy," I whispered to Popcorn. "We're going to have some fun."

Chapter 2
Too Many Tricks!

Mrs Hambone stood in the middle of the ring, watching us trot. She clasped her riding crop like a ringmaster at a circus.

Popcorn and I trotted past her. "Do I have to ride sitting down?" I asked.

Mrs Hambone gave me a worried look. "What.do you mean, Sophie?"

"I could ride standing up," I said.

Before Mrs Hambone could say anything, I quickly kicked off my riding boots.

Then, I slowly stood up on the saddle. Popcorn and I had done this trick hundreds of times. I stretched my arms wide and bent my knees. Good old Popcorn trotted smoothly around the ring.

The other riders quickly pulled their ponies out of our way. Their eyes were wide with amazement.

"Wow!" said the girl on the grey pony.

Next, I gripped the saddle with both hands and lifted my feet into the air. My toes pointed at the clouds as the world turned upside down.

Mrs Hambone's face went a bright shade of purple. "Stop horsing around!" she said. "This is a pony club, not a circus."

Soon, trotting practice came to an end.

"Everyone gather round," said Mrs Hambone. "I have some exciting news about the next gymkhana."

"What's a gymkhana?" I asked.

"It's a fun day that all the pony clubs in the area take part in each year," she told me. "There are all sorts of riding competitions."

"And lots of ribbons to be won," said a girl with long plaits.

"Silver Saddles is the best pony club," said another girl. "Our ponies always win the most ribbons."

"I'm sure Popcorn will win one," I said, feeling excited for the first time that day.

I couldn't wait to show everyone that Popcorn really was a superstar!

Chapter 3

The First Event

It was the day of the gymkhana. Flags fluttered in the breeze as the ponies lined up outside the show ring. Their manes were neatly brushed and their coats shone.

"The first event is the Best Led Pony," said the head judge, Mr Grimble. "Ponies will be judged for how well they walk around the ring."

This will be easy for Popcorn, I thought. *Just as long as he behaves himself.*

One by one, the ponies were led into the ring. Their owners walked them around the ring once and then stood in front of the judges.

14

Soon, it was Popcorn's turn. I tugged his lead rope and led him into the ring. He walked a few steps and stopped still.

I pulled on Popcorn's rope, but he refused to budge.

"Come on, boy," I said.

I tugged harder and dragged Popcorn a few steps forward. His hooves dug into the ground like a cartoon horse.

Mr Grimble looked at his watch and gave a loud sigh.

I tugged on the rope again. This time, Popcorn lifted his head and snorted. The crowd laughed.

Popcorn's ears pricked up. He liked to make people laugh. He did a couple of dance steps and the crowd laughed again.

In front of us stood a judge with frizzy hair and lots of pearls. Popcorn danced towards her and blew air into her face.

The crowd cheered and laughed. The judge began to laugh, too, but suddenly her face changed and she let out a howl of pain.

"Ow!" she shrieked, pointing to the ground.

Popcorn's big fat hoof was planted right on top of her shiny shoe. Oops!

Popcorn did not win a ribbon for the Best Led Pony. The prize went to a boy with a brown pony that was so quiet it might as well have been asleep.

"Never mind," I said to Popcorn, flicking dust from his neck. "The next event is the Neatest Pony. You'll win that hands down."

Chapter 4

Cheers for Popcorn

Dozens of squeaky-clean ponies lined up in a row. Everyone wanted to win the ribbon for the Neatest Pony. I snuck a comb out of my pocket and combed Popcorn's tail and mane. I even combed his eyelashes.

Popcorn really did look like the neatest pony in the Neatest Pony event.

I was sure we would win a ribbon this time.

The crowd was silent as the judge walked along the line. All the ponies stood perfectly still, even Popcorn. Coats were inspected for dirt, and manes were examined for tangles.

As the judge walked towards us, I gave him my best smile. He looked all over Popcorn's neck and body and then strolled around to look at his tail.

Popcorn didn't like people standing behind him. He whirled around and faced the judge. The judge tried again, springing towards Popcorn's rear end. Soon Popcorn was spinning in circles and so was the judge.

Half the crowd cheered on Popcorn. The other half cheered on the judge.

Suddenly, Popcorn stopped still. "Hurray!" shouted the judge, and grabbed Popcorn's tail.

But all that spinning must have upset Popcorn's belly. He let out a terrible smell.

The judge screwed up his nose and tried to wave the smell away. People in the stands laughed.

Then, the judge swung around and gave the ribbon for the Neatest Pony to a fat pony with a sleek, shiny mane.

Oh, dear!

After that, there were more events and more ribbons given out. However, Popcorn didn't win any of them. He trotted around the ring when he should have been walking backwards. He nibbled the judge's ear when he should have been standing still. He even chewed one of the ribbons hanging from the judge's arm.

Every pony from the Silver Saddles Pony Club had won a ribbon, except for Popcorn.

Mrs Hambone looked worried. "There is only one event left," she told me. "It will be Popcorn's last chance to win a ribbon."

"Don't worry," I said, firmly. "Popcorn is sure to win."

Chapter 5

Popcorn's Last Chance

The last competition was for the pony with the whitest teeth. The other riders in the Silver Saddles Pony Club gathered around Popcorn. One girl took out a tissue and began to rub Popcorn's teeth.

"It's Popcorn's turn to win," she said, kindly.

Poor Popcorn. He was used to being a star, and now he was dunce of the class.

"Come on," I said to Popcorn. "You can do it!"

Mr Grimble was the judge for the last event. The other judges were sitting down with sore feet or pony dribble in their hair. Mr Grimble moved slowly down the line, peering into pony mouths, one by one.

"Open wide," he said, when he reached Popcorn. Popcorn clamped his teeth shut. He stared at a passing fly.

"Come on, boy," said the judge. "Let's see those shiny teeth."

Popcorn's eyes rolled wildly. "Wait!" I cried. I took a carrot out of my pocket and waved it under Popcorn's nose. He loved juicy carrots. He spread his lips into a big pony grin and showed off his teeth.

"What lovely clean teeth!" said Mr Grimble, as Popcorn chomped on the carrot. "I think we've found our winner."

At that moment, the fly tickled Popcorn's nose. He shook his head and snorted. Bits of carrot flew out of his mouth and landed in Mr Grimble's curly hair.

The crowd roared with laughter.

"That was your last chance," I told Popcorn, when Mr Grimble chose another pony as the winner. "You blew it, big time."

Chapter 6

Popcorn, the Superstar

Slowly, I led Popcorn towards the gate leading out of the ring. He looked naked compared to the other ponies – he was the only one without a ribbon around his neck.

"Never mind," called someone from the stands. "Popcorn gave us all a good laugh."

Even Mrs Hambone managed to smile. "That pony should be in a circus," she said.

I nodded. A pony club was not the right place for a smart pony like Popcorn. He needed to be appreciated.

"Ladies and gentlemen, boys and girls," called Mr Grimble through his megaphone. "The judges have decided to award one final ribbon."

We all stopped still and listened.

"The last prize is for the Most Entertaining Pony. This prize goes to –"

"Popcorn!" cried the crowd.

"Popcorn!" cried Mr Grimble.

Popcorn trotted towards the judge and bowed his head for the ribbon. Then he pranced about the ring, legs high.

"Well done, Popcorn," called the riders from the Silver Saddles Pony Club. "What a star!"

"He's a superstar," I said, with a grin.